Dear Parent:
Your child's love of reading starts here!

Every child learns to read in a different way and at his or her own speed. Some go back and forth between reading levels and read favorite books again and again. Others read through each level in order. You can help your young reader improve and become more confident by encouraging his or her own interests and abilities. From books your child reads with you to the first books he or she reads alone, there are I Can Read Books for every stage of reading:

SHARED READING
Basic language, word repetition, and whimsical illustrations, ideal for sharing with your emergent reader

BEGINNING READING
Short sentences, familiar words, and simple concepts for children eager to read on their own

READING WITH HELP
Engaging stories, longer sentences, and language play for developing readers

READING ALONE
Complex plots, challenging vocabulary, and high-interest topics for the independent reader

ADVANCED READING
Short paragraphs, chapters, and exciting themes for the perfect bridge to chapter books

I Can Read Books have introduced children to the joy of reading since 1957. Featuring award-winning authors and illustrators and a fabulous cast of beloved characters, I Can Read Books set the standard for beginning readers.

A lifetime of discovery begins with the magical words **"I Can Read!"**

Visit www.icanread.com for information
on enriching your child's reading experience.

I Can Read Book® is a trademark of HarperCollins Publishers.

Superman: A Giant Attack
Copyright © 2015 DC Comics.
SUPERMAN and all related characters and elements are trademarks of and © DC Comics.
(s15)

HARP33135
Manufactured in the U.S.A. No part of this book may be used or reproduced in any manner whatsoever without written permission except in the case of brief quotations embodied in critical articles and reviews. For information address HarperCollins Children's Books, a division of HarperCollins Publishers, 195 Broadway, New York, NY 10007.
www.harpercollinschildrens.com

Library of Congress catalog card number: 2014947578
ISBN 978-0-06-234488-5

Book design by Victor Joseph Ochoa

16 17 18 19 20   LSCC   10 9 8 7 6 5 4   ❖   First Edition

I Can Read! READING WITH HELP 2

SUPERMAN™

A GIANT ATTACK

by Donald Lemke
pictures by Lee Ferguson

Superman created by Jerry Siegel and Joe Shuster
By special arrangement with the Jerry Siegel family.

HARPER
An Imprint of HarperCollinsPublishers

SUPERMAN

Superman, also known as the Man of Steel, has many amazing powers. He was born on the planet Krypton.

RED KRYPTONITE

A form of Kryptonite that has unexpected and temporary effects on Kryptonians.

S.T.A.R. LABS

S.T.A.R. Labs is a research facility located in Metropolis. Scientists at the laboratory invent high-tech weapons and gadgets.

LEX LUTHOR

Lex Luthor is a wealthy Metropolis businessman. He is Superman's enemy.

ZOD AND FAORA

Zod and Faora are criminals from Superman's home planet. They were sent to the Phantom Zone before Krypton was destroyed.

PHANTOM ZONE

The Phantom Zone is a prison dimension for criminals from Krypton. Prisoners travel to and from this prison through a Phantom Zone Projector.

DING! A golden elevator opened
on the top floor of LexCorp Tower.
Lex Luthor stepped out, and
a nervous scientist greeted him.
"Is everything ready?" Lex asked
the former S.T.A.R. Labs employee.

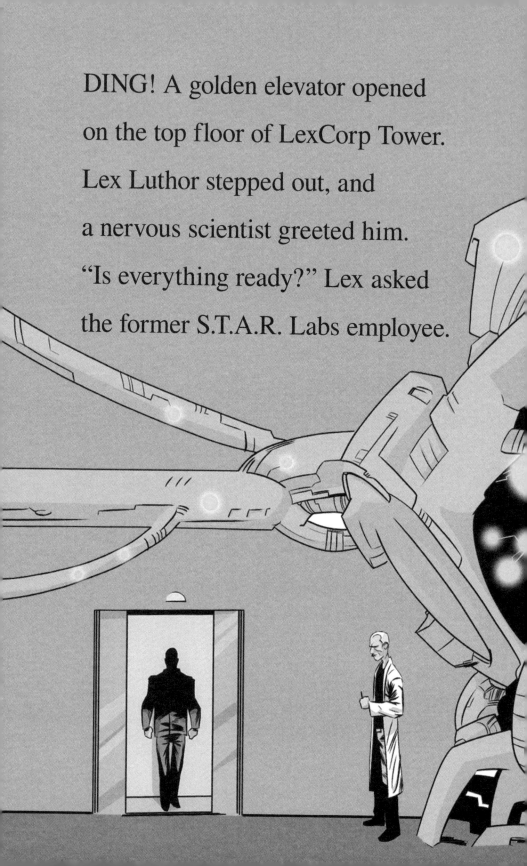

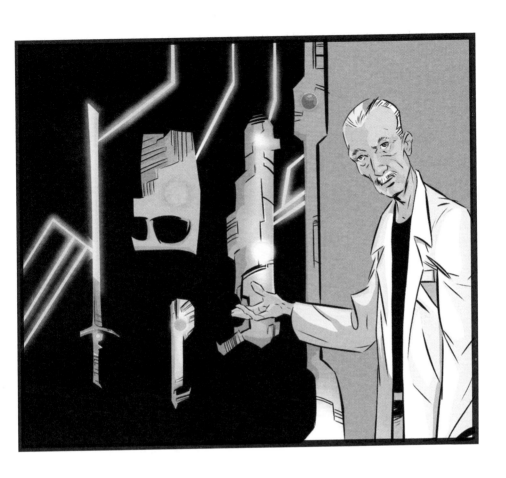

The scientist nodded and pointed

toward a large glass display case.

High-tech gadgets glowed inside.

Each device had one purpose:

to destroy Superman.

Lex removed a device from the case.

"A Phantom Zone Projector, sir,"

said the scientist.

"We built one at S.T.A.R. Labs.

Yours is better.

And more expensive."

Lex grabbed the scientist.

"I'd better get what I paid for,"

said the businessman.

Then he turned on the device.

BAM! Suddenly, two Phantom Zone

criminals appeared in front of them.

"Finally we're free!" said Zod.

"I wouldn't say 'free,'"
Lex told the criminals.

"What do you want?" asked Faora.

"Superman," he growled.

"Gladly," replied the evil duo.

"Excellent," said Lex,

grabbing a rocket launcher

from the case.

"Then meet me on the roof."

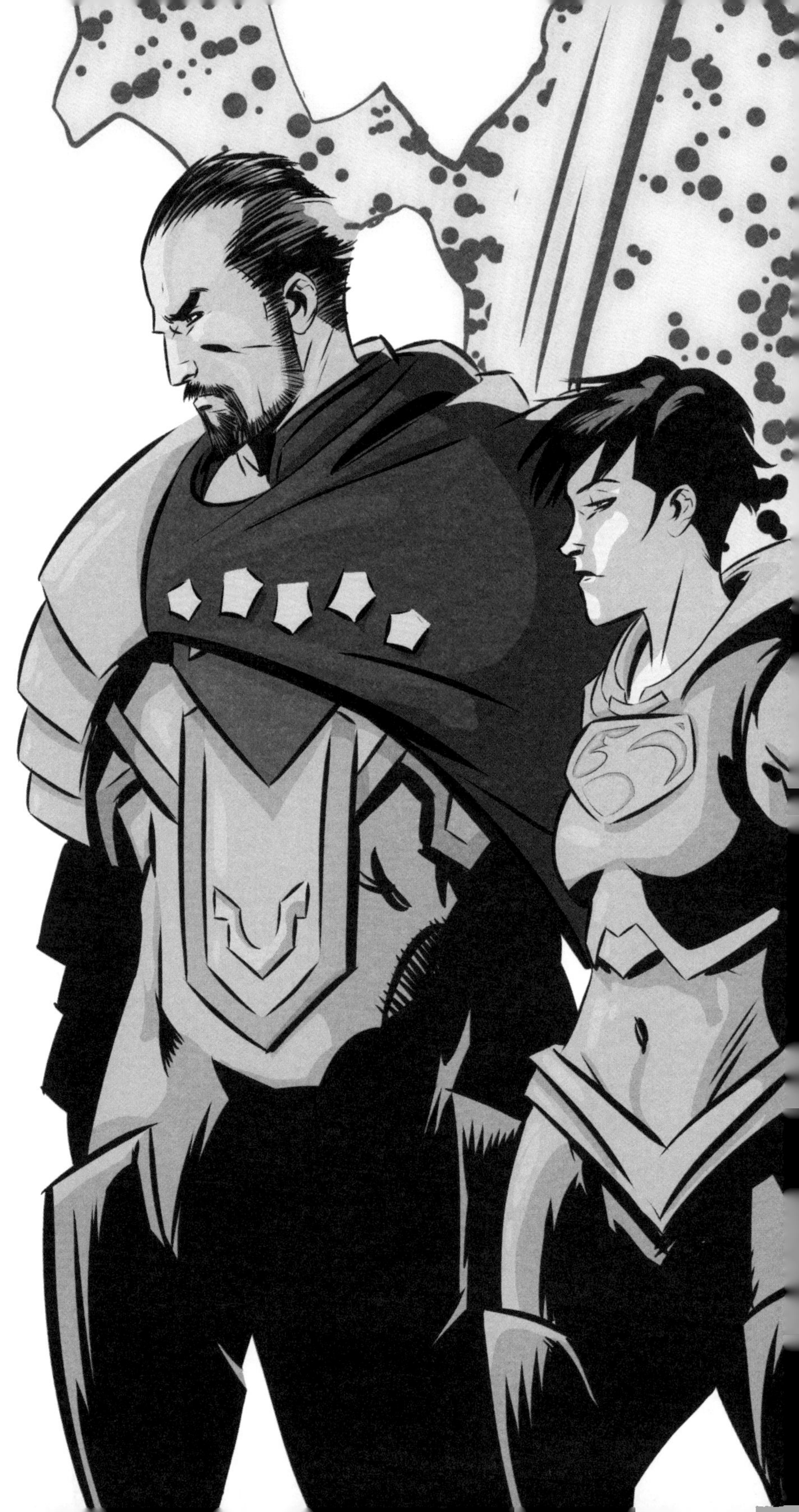

"Now what?" asked Faora.
Lex pointed the rocket launcher
toward the clear blue sky above.
"We start with a bang!" he said,
pulling the trigger.

KA-BOOM! A silver missile
streaked toward a nearby building.
Without delay, a blue-and-red figure
appeared beside it . . . Superman!

With super-speed, the Man of Steel
soared behind the missile
and grabbed the tail.
"Time to put the brakes on this
situation," the super hero said.

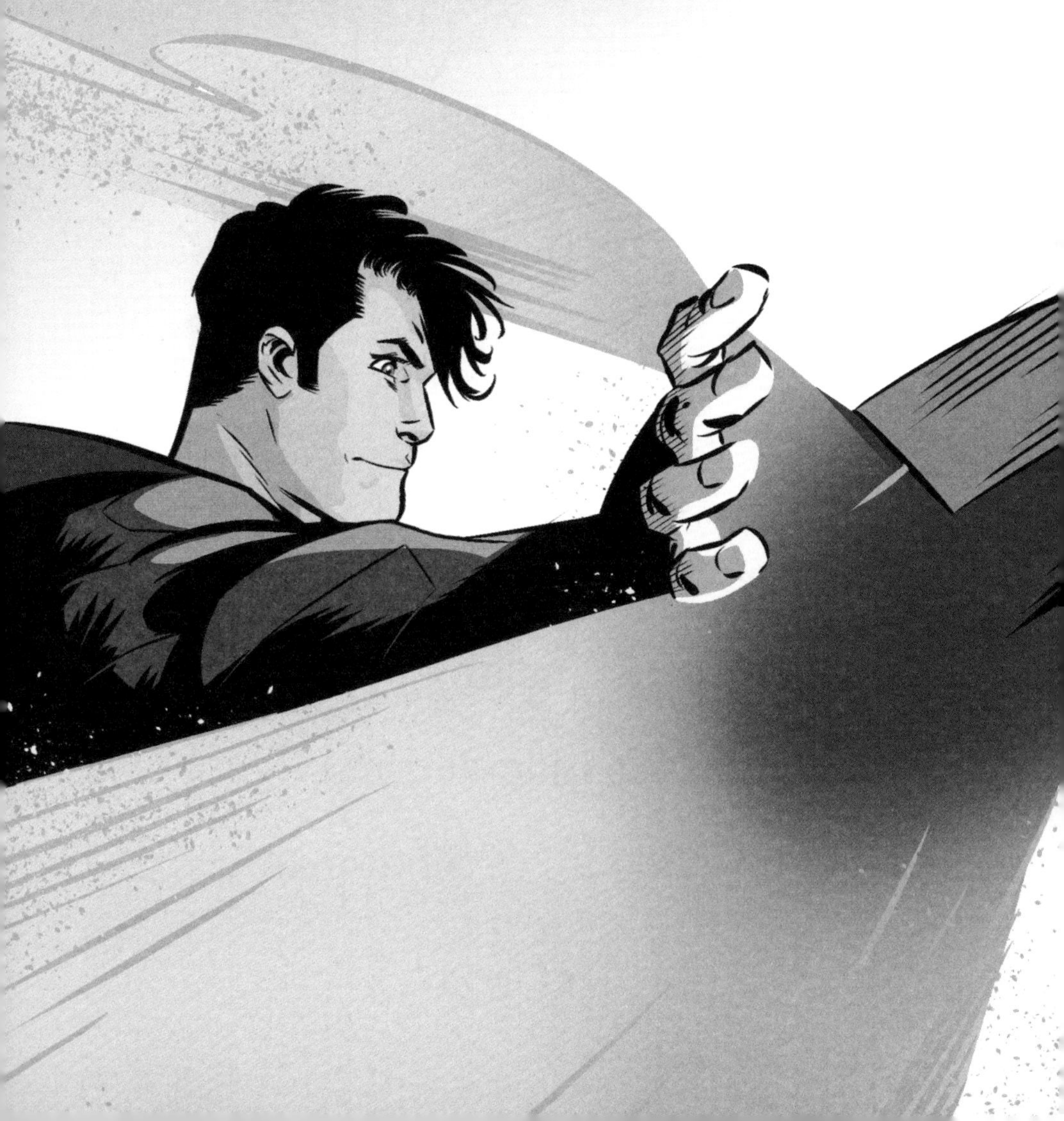

BLAM! The missile suddenly exploded in a blast of red light. The super hero fell from the sky, crashing through the thick concrete sidewalk below.

"What on earth is that weapon?"

Faora asked Lex.

"You won't find this weapon

on Earth," he replied.

"I've made the newest form

of Red Kryptonite."

On the ground below,

Superman grew . . . and grew!

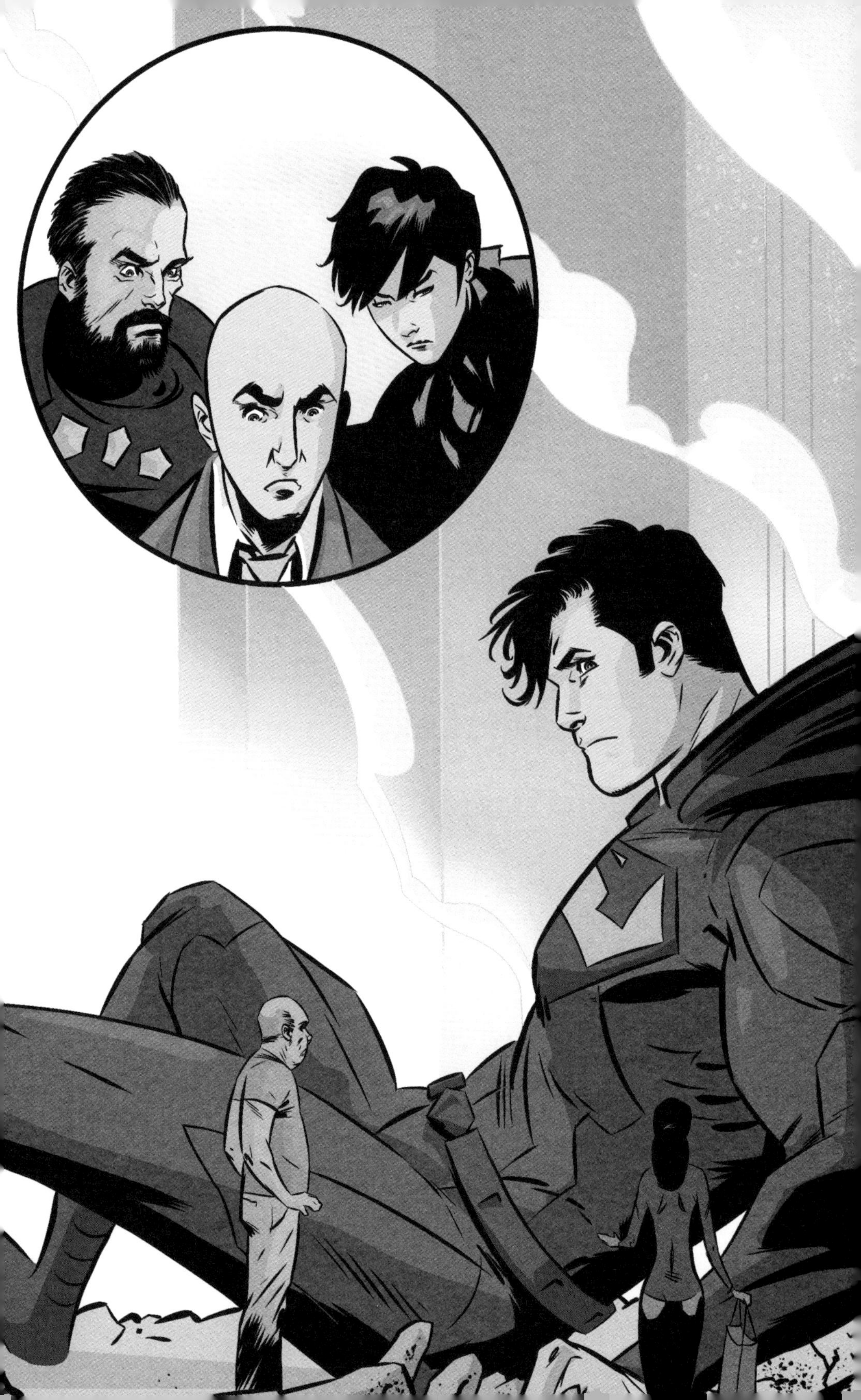

"You fool!" shouted Zod.

"Do you know what kind of mess you've made?"

"A *giant* mess!" Faora answered.

The Man of Steel stood taller than the LexCorp building.

The hero stared at the tiny villains with his giant red eyes.

"You're all in big trouble," joked Superman.

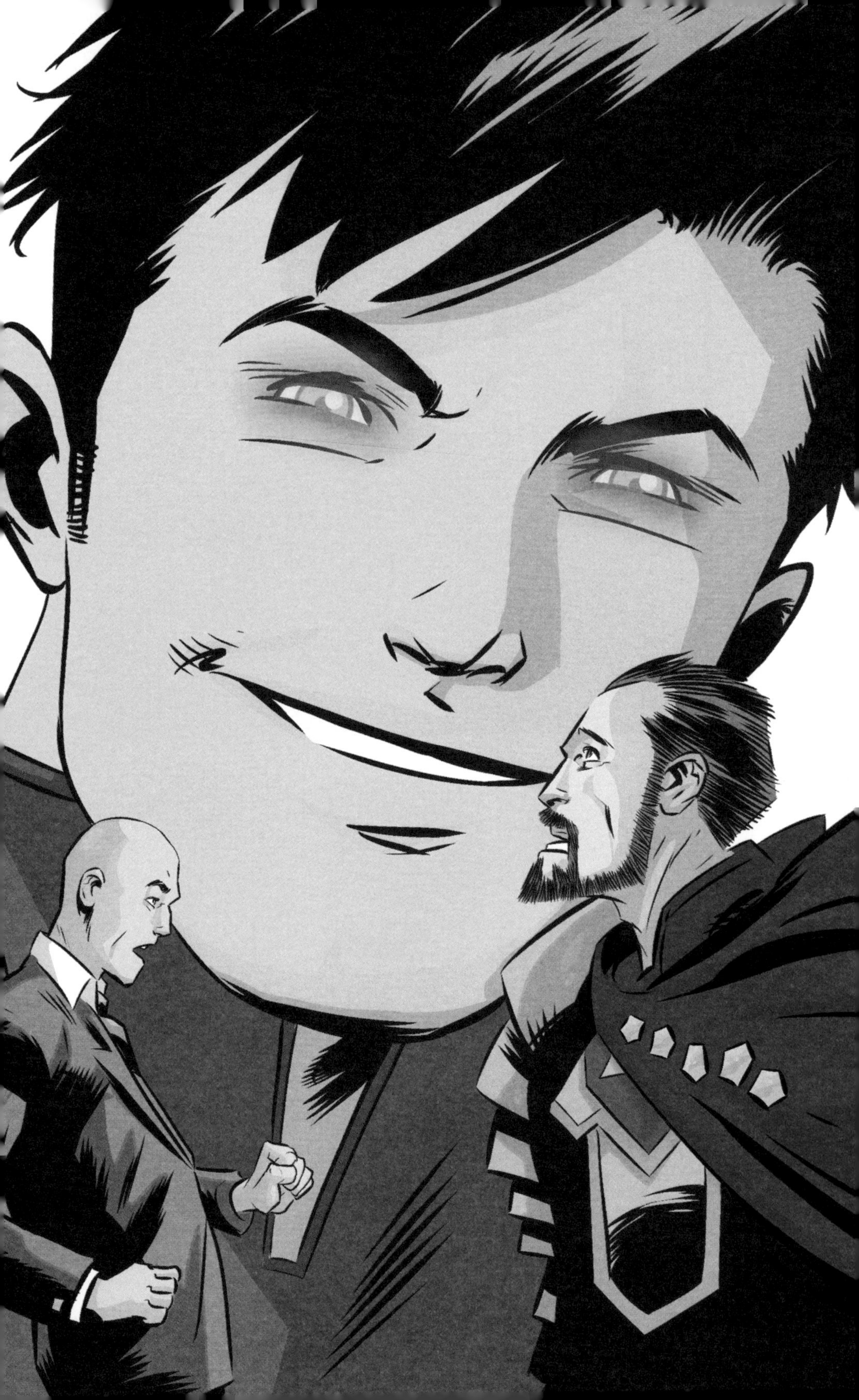

Zod and Faora circled Superman's head like two pesky bees.

"The bigger they are," Zod began.

"The harder they fall," added Faora.

The hero raised his huge palm.

"Bug off!" Superman shouted.

THWAP! He swatted the villains in midair, sending them crashing into nearby buildings.

The evil duo flew

at Superman again.

They punched him over and over

with their teeny, pin-size fists.

"I'm growing tired of you two,"

Superman said, letting out a yawn.

A gust of super-breath

escaped his mouth.

The villains fell to the ground,

covered in a layer of ice.

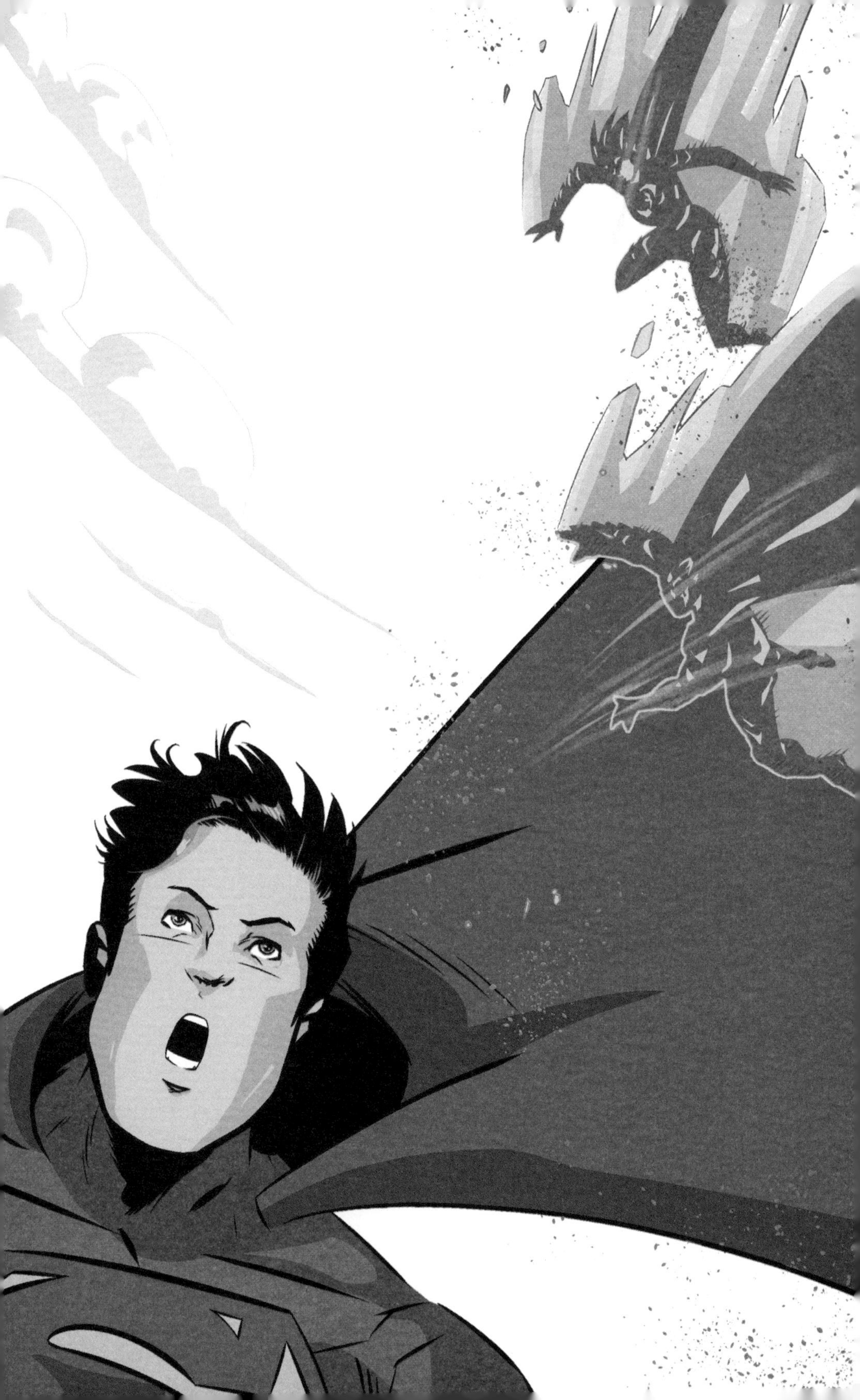

Zod and Faora quickly flew back

to the LexCorp building.

"Get back out here!" cried Lex.

"You still owe me for your freedom!"

"Until that Red K wears off," said Faora,

"we'd be crazy to stay and fight him."

"Then our deal is dead," said Lex, starting the Phantom Zone Projector. With the push of a button, he sent the evil duo back to their prison.

Superman's giant finger suddenly
smashed through a nearby window.
Lex hid behind the display case.
The super hero searched the room
with his X-ray vision.
He quickly spotted his enemy.

The Man of Steel blasted the case
with his heat vision. FWOOSH!
In an instant,
Lex's gadgets melted
into a red-hot puddle
on the floor.

"What have you done?" Lex asked
the scientist standing nearby.

"What you wanted, sir," he replied.

"How long will this last?" said Lex.

"If my Red K formula was correct,"
answered the scientist, "two days."

The giant Superman grabbed

Lex and the scientist.

"If we last that long," Lex added.

Superman pulled the men
into the air.

"S.T.A.R. Labs' secrets
are safe again," he said, smiling.

Suddenly the hero began shrinking.

Lex and the scientist dropped

to the rooftop.

Superman returned to normal size.

"This giant mess is all your fault!"
Lex shouted at the scientist
as a policeman led them away.
"Don't worry," said the super hero.
"You'll both pay for this mistake."